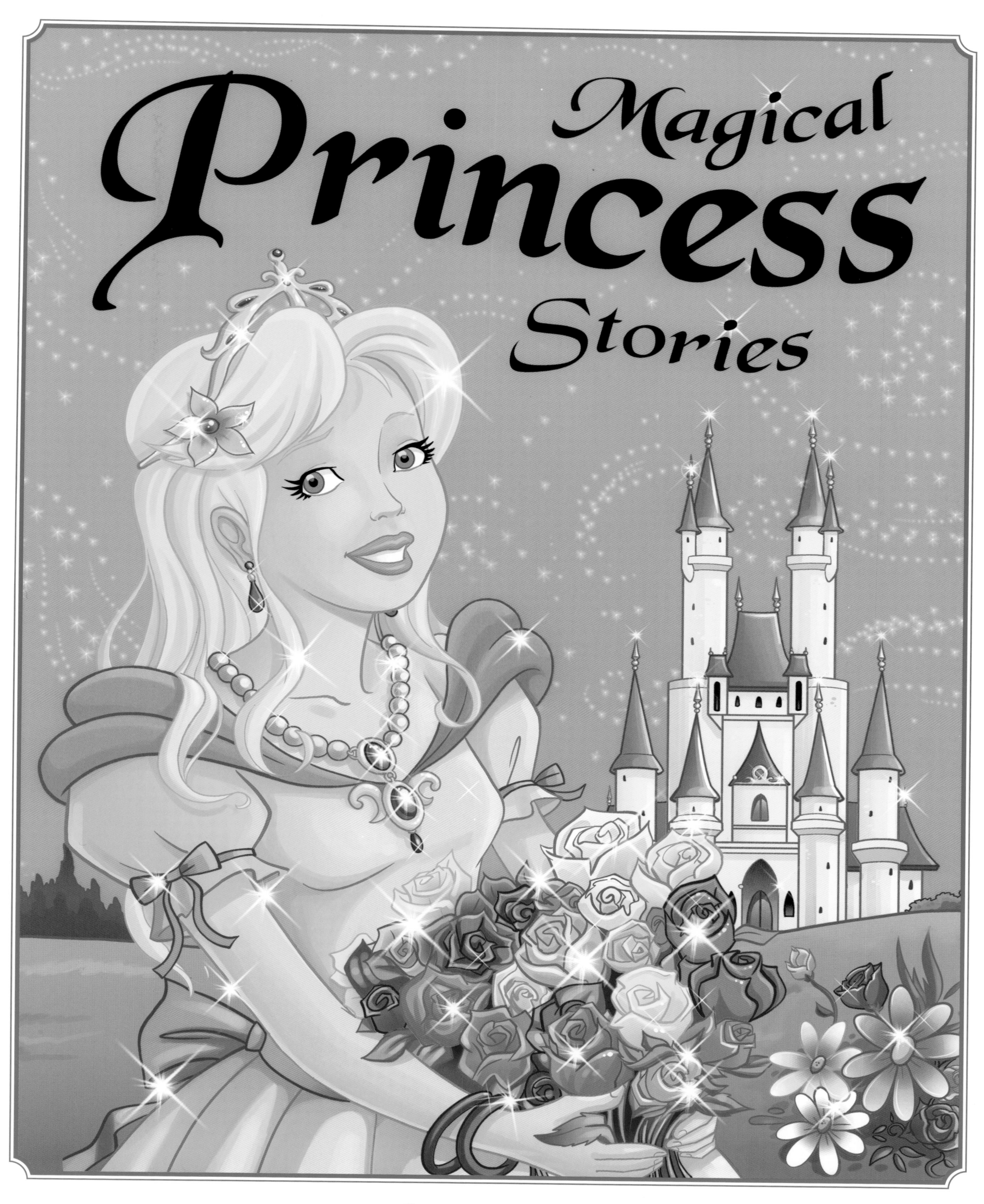

ENGLAND LE8 0HG

Contents

Cinderella

Cinderella was a good girl. She worked hard to care for her stepmother and stepsisters. She cleaned and cooked, and washed their beautiful clothes. But the stepsisters were wicked. Instead of saying thank you, they were mean to Cinderella. She wore rags instead of fancy dresses, and slept on the dirty kitchen floor.

The wicked sisters were invited to a grand ball at the royal palace. "Prince Charming is looking for a bride!" they screeched.

"I bet he chooses me!"

"No, me!" they argued together.

Cinderella helped them put on their finest clothes and then sadly waved them goodbye.

Poor Cinders sat alone, wishing she could go to the ball. Then she gasped as a shining light appeared, and transformed into a fairy!

"You shall go to the ball!" twinkled the fairy, and waved her wand. Cinderella's rags turned into a wonderful ball gown, and her hair was decorated with the finest jewels.

"Come outside..." said the fairy, where she waved her wand once more. Four scuttling mice, a frog, and a pumpkin magically became a sparkling coach and horses.

"There is just one rule," said the fairy. "At midnight, the magic will end. You must leave the ball before the clock strikes twelve."

Prince Charming danced with Cinderella all night. He didn't talk to anybody else. Then Cinderella heard the clock begin to chime. "Midnight!" she thought, and ran away.

Prince Charming followed her, but she had disappeared. All he could see was a delicate glass shoe. He called his valet and said, "Help me find the girl who wore this shoe – I want to marry her!"

Prince Charming travelled for miles to see who was the wearer of the glass shoe. At Cinderella's house, her wicked sisters could not squeeze their feet into the shoe. "Will you try?" he asked Cinderella.

And of course, the shoe was a perfect fit. Prince Charming had found his bride and their marriage was a long and happy one.

The Swan Princess

One sunny summer morning, Princess Sophia went out to play. She loved to run to the lake in their palace grounds and watch the dragonflies dart around the rushes. She was an only child, and dearly wished she had a sister to play with.

As she lay on her tummy and watched a bug climb a blade of grass, she heard a strange tinkling noise. It didn't sound like water, or the wind...it sounded like a tiny bell. She stared at the lawn and listened carefully.

There it was again! And then she saw what was making the noise. A tiny fairy flitted through the leaves, looking like a dainty dragonfly with silvery wings. Princess Sophia gasped.

"Don't be afraid!" twinkled the little fairy, landing next to Sophia's nose. "I have come to ask for your help!"

Princess Sophia nodded and smiled. She was scared that her voice might be loud enough to make the fairy's ears hurt.

The fairy flew onto Sophia's finger and pointed her wand at the lake. She explained that the smallest swan that lived there wasn't a swan at all, but a lonely orphan from a faraway land. A wicked sorcerer had cast a spell and banished her to Sophia's garden.

"All you have to do is take her from your lake and place her in your royal bathtub," said the fairy. "But be careful you don't drown – and don't tell anyone, ever."

Princess Sophia spotted a canoe at the lake's edge. Was she brave enough to sail in it alone? Of course she was! She climbed in and carefully paddled to the island in the middle of the lake. Her beautiful dress was all wet and muddy but she didn't mind.

As she sailed next to the swans, some of them hissed and flapped their huge wings. Sophia ignored them. She found the smallest swan and gently placed it in her boat. It looked frightened, but didn't flap at all.

Princess Sophia returned to the shore and ran excitedly to her bathroom. She filled the tub with water and lifted the swan into it. For the second time that day, Sophia gasped as the swan disappeared and a girl took its place. She hugged Sophia tightly and thanked her over and over. How exciting – now Sophia had a brand new friend!

Snow White and the Seven Dwarves

Snow White was a beautiful princess, but she was not happy. Her mother had died and the new queen hated Snow White with all her heart.

The evil queen was very vain. Every day she would ask her enchanted mirror, "Mirror, mirror, on the wall, who is the fairest of us all?" Every day the mirror promised that the queen was the fairest in the whole land.

As Snow White grew older, she became even more beautiful. The wicked queen was livid! Her mirror now told her that Snow White was the fairest in the land. The queen ordered her huntsman to kill Snow White.

The huntsman was kind, and he took Snow White to a safe place in the forest where she could hide. Snow White found a cute little cottage furnished with a table and seven chairs. There were seven little beds in the bedroom. Snow White was so tired she curled up on one bed and fell fast asleep.

She awoke to find seven pairs of eyes watching her. The cottage belonged to seven dwarves, who said she was welcome to stay with them. She cleaned and cooked and was very happy there. The dwarves loved Snow White very much.

One day, the magic mirror said that Snow White was still the most beautiful. The queen flew into a rage. She disguised herself and went to see Snow White with a gift: a lovely red apple.

Snow White took one bite and fell down, poisoned. The evil queen ran away, laughing. That night, the dwarves found Snow White on the floor. After crying and sobbing, they decided to put her in a glass coffin so her beauty wasn't hidden away.

A passing prince saw the dwarves at work. "She is so beautiful!" he exclaimed, and kissed her hand. His kiss broke the spell that had been cast by the evil queen. The dwarves cheered as Snow White woke up, and the prince instantly asked her to be his wife.

A Pony Princess

Nina loved horses, and horses loved Nina. Sadly, Nina's family was extremely poor, and they could never afford a horse of her own. Her mother, father, sisters and brothers all worked hard each day just to earn money for their own food.

Nina had a job at the royal palace. She worked in the kitchen, doing all the dirty jobs the cook didn't like to do. She helped with the cleaning, as she was small enough to reach places the maid couldn't reach. Whenever she could, she helped at the stables. She didn't care what jobs they gave her there. She just loved being close to the horses.

Sometimes, the prince came to see his favourite horse, Majestic. Nina hid and listened to him talk to the stallion. "Oh, Majestic! You are my best friend in the whole world! You're the only one who really listens to me," sighed the prince.

One day, the prince spotted Nina in the stalls. He was a very kind young man, and he offered to let Nina ride his horse.

As Nina trotted around the yard, smiling her biggest smile, a loud bang made Majestic bolt. He galloped straight towards the nearby forest at top speed, and Nina could do nothing to make him stop. Eventually, he halted in a clearing.

As Nina's heart stopped pounding, she saw a ghostly white shape between the trees. A unicorn! The beautiful creature trotted over and nuzzled up to the horse. It looked at Nina and without even speaking, it put words into her mind.

"You are the chosen one," Nina felt in her head. "I shall grant you three wishes!"

Straight away, three thoughts flashed into Nina's brain. She wanted her family to have more money, she wanted a pony of her own, and she wished the prince would be her friend. "It is done!" thought the unicorn.

That year, all of Nina's wishes came true. Her family was no longer poor, and the prince fell head over heels in love with her and asked her to marry him. And of course, that meant she had plenty of ponies to call her own!

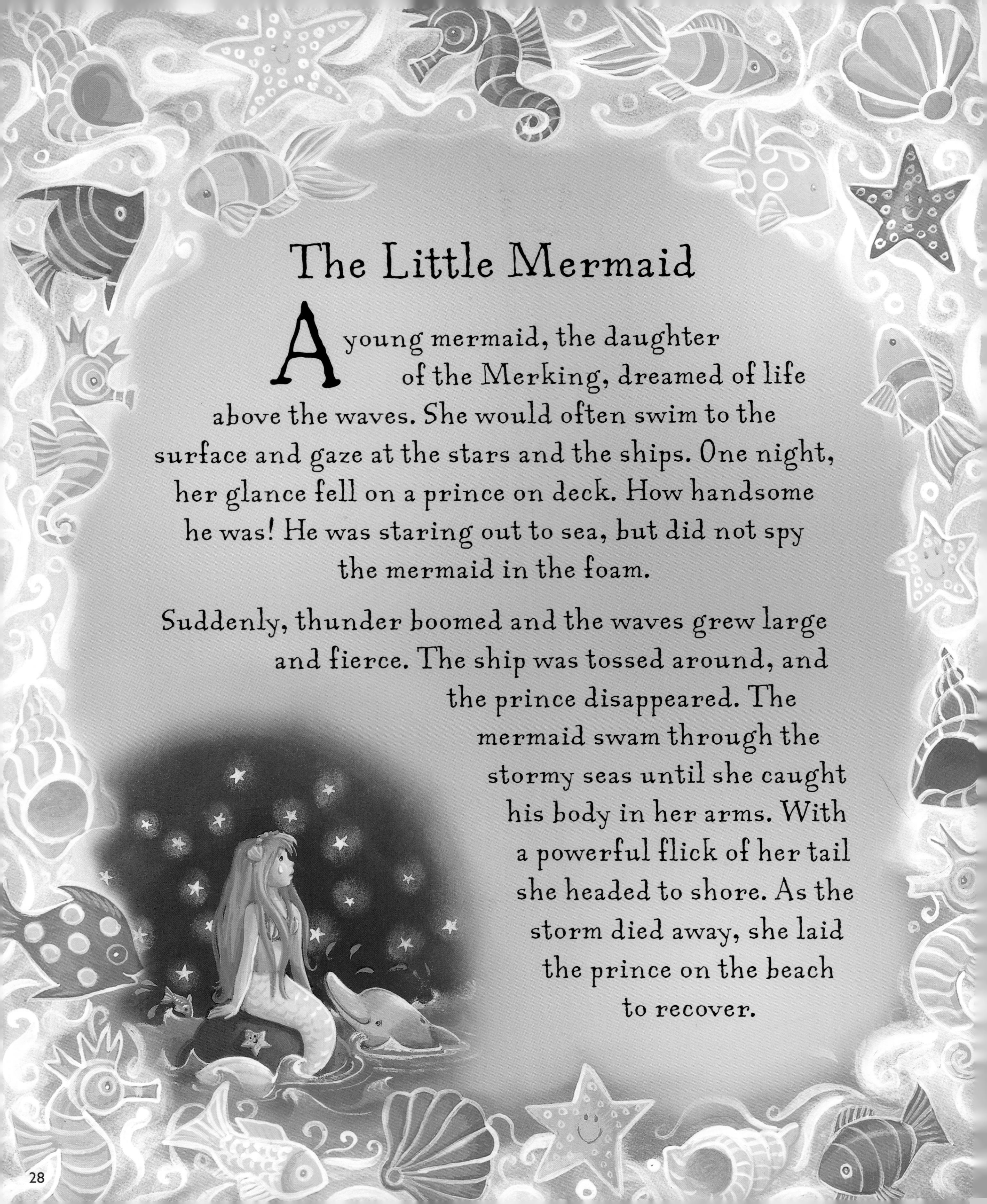

The Little Mermaid

A young mermaid, the daughter of the Merking, dreamed of life above the waves. She would often swim to the surface and gaze at the stars and the ships. One night, her glance fell on a prince on deck. How handsome he was! He was staring out to sea, but did not spy the mermaid in the foam.

Suddenly, thunder boomed and the waves grew large and fierce. The ship was tossed around, and the prince disappeared. The mermaid swam through the stormy seas until she caught his body in her arms. With a powerful flick of her tail she headed to shore. As the storm died away, she laid the prince on the beach to recover.

For many days, the mermaid dreamed of the prince. She desperately wanted to grow legs and live on the land with him. The mermaid swam into the murky depths to ask the evil sea witch for her help.

"Oh, my pretty one!" the sea witch gurgled. "This potion will give you legs, but be warned. Every step you take will be like walking on knives. If the prince takes any other wife, you will return to the sea as the foam on the waves. And it will cost you your beautiful voice..."

The mermaid was so desperate that she agreed to pay the price. As she swam away, her tail became legs, and she struggled to the shore. The pain was so great that she fainted, and awoke in the sunshine. Staring down at her was the prince, who gently scooped her up in his arms and carried her to his palace.

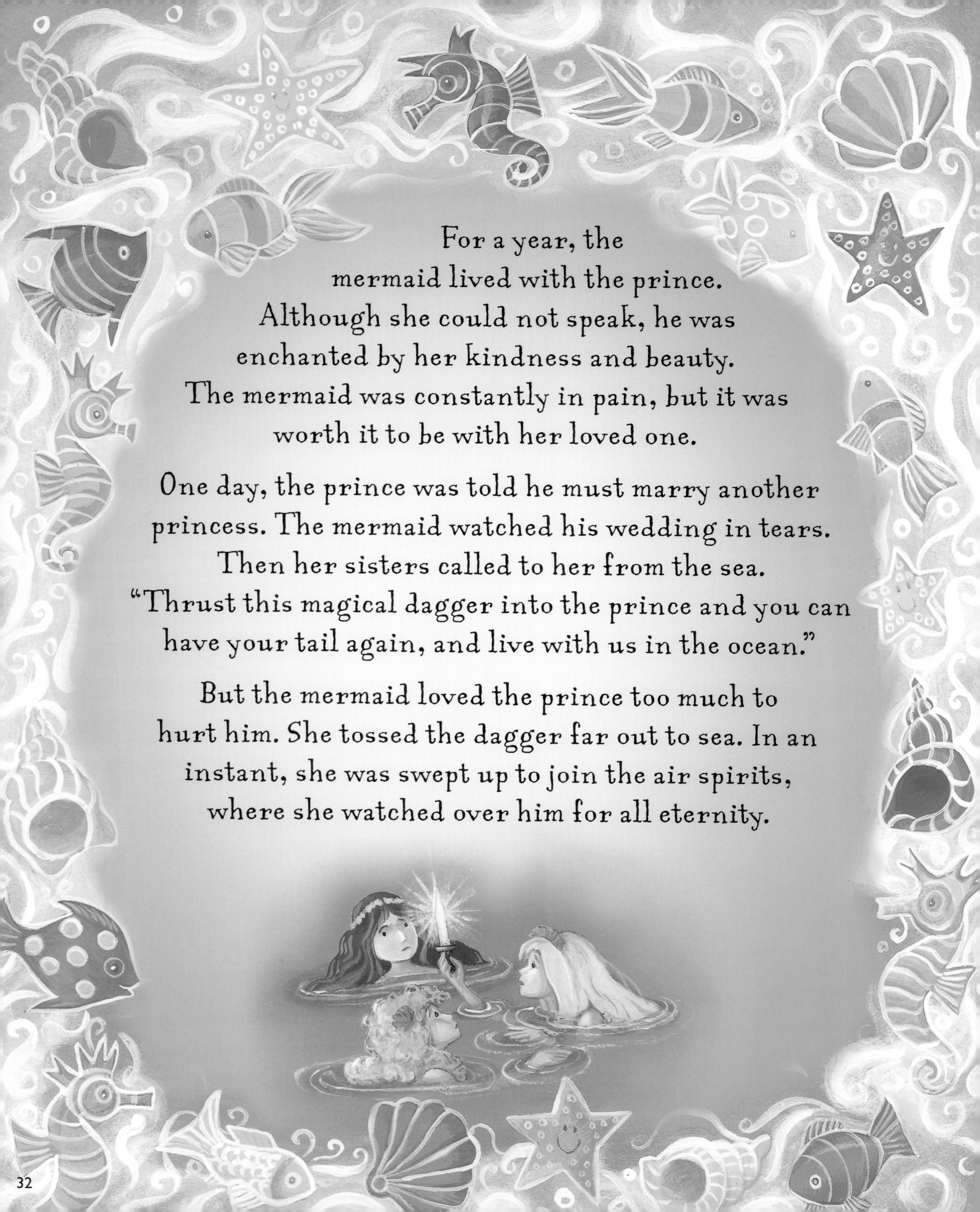

For a year, the mermaid lived with the prince. Although she could not speak, he was enchanted by her kindness and beauty. The mermaid was constantly in pain, but it was worth it to be with her loved one.

One day, the prince was told he must marry another princess. The mermaid watched his wedding in tears. Then her sisters called to her from the sea. "Thrust this magical dagger into the prince and you can have your tail again, and live with us in the ocean."

But the mermaid loved the prince too much to hurt him. She tossed the dagger far out to sea. In an instant, she was swept up to join the air spirits, where she watched over him for all eternity.

The Dancing Princess

Princess Tanika was a beautiful dancer. Every day, her dance teacher came to the palace to help her practice her steps. Each week, Tanika danced in front of her mother and father to show them how good she was getting.

One day, as she swirled and twirled around her parents' room, her father spoke to her. "Tanika, my most adored daughter," he began, "I think that you should show the whole nation how talented you are. We shall have a dancing competition, here in the palace! Anyone can enter, boy or girl, and you shall see if you truly are the greatest dancer in the country."

Princess Tanika clapped her hands in delight and ran away to tell her teacher.

On the day of the dance competition, Tanika hung out of her bedroom window, watching as hundreds of children arrived to take part. Suddenly, she heard a whistle. She gasped as a young boy swooshed past her nose, travelling on a flying carpet!

The boy flew back again and hovered outside her room. "Who are you?" she whispered.

"I am Prince Tanak," he proclaimed. "And I bet I am a better dancer than you!"

Princess Tanika's eyes widened in surprise. "Well, we'll see about that!" she said. She put on her dancing slippers and pirouetted out of her room.

The dance competition lasted for hours. The king chose six dancers to be in the final. Princess Tanika was not surprised to see that Prince Tanak was still on the floor.

The prince danced over to Tanika and took her hand. He spun her around and around, and the audience gasped to see them dance together. One by one, the others stopped dancing to watch the couple. Their feet moved so fast it was as if they had a spell cast on them.

Eventually, Princess Tanika dropped the prince's hand. "I give in," she said. "You are better than me, and I am just too tired to dance any more. You must be the winner!"

"Then that means you are the true winner," said the prince. "For I have magic to help me, and you dance without it. Let the whole world know that Princess Tanika is the best dancer this country has ever seen!"

Sleeping Beauty

The king and queen of a far off land were blessed with a baby daughter. They loved her very much, and threw a lavish party for her. Everyone was invited, except Carabosse, the evil fairy.

The guests lined up with presents for the baby princess. The fairies gave special gifts such as beauty, brains and kindness. Then Carabosse appeared and pushed to the front of the queue. "My gift is this: on her sixteenth birthday she will prick her finger and die!"

The guests gasped and the queen fainted. Then a kind fairy stepped forward. "I still have my gift," she said. "I cannot undo that curse, but instead of death, she will only sleep for a hundred years."

Instantly, the king ruled that all sharp objects were banned from his land. The princess grew to be kind and clever, as the fairies had said.

On her sixteenth birthday, the princess woke early and heard a strange noise. She found an old woman spinning thread. Bending to pick up a stray spindle, the princess pricked her finger and fell to the floor in a faint.

The king was called at once, and carried his daughter to her bed. As soon as he laid her on it, he also fell into an enchanted slumber. Everyone in the castle slept too, from the cook's cat to the chief of the guards.

For a hundred years, nobody awoke.
Thorny bushes grew wild and covered the whole castle so that no-one could reach it.

On the last day of the hundred years, a young prince rode by. He had heard stories about the castle, and was amazed to see it suddenly appear as the thorns magically fell away.

He rode through the front gate past all the sleeping people. "I wonder if the princess really exists?" he thought. Exploring each room, he found a beautiful young girl in fine clothes.

"This must be her!" he whispered, and kissed her on the cheek.

The spell was broken, and everyone awoke. The prince and princess fell in love, and Carabosse was never seen again.

A Fairy Princess

The sun was twinkling in the sky when Princess Fayette flew from her house to play outside. It was still early, and dew covered the cobwebs where her favourite spider lived.

"Good morning, Mrs Spinnikins!" she sang. "I'm going to play in the forest today!"

Mrs Spinnikins waved two arms at her, and Fayette flew into the trees. She darted here and there, chasing woodpeckers and listening to the squirrels chatter to each other. She followed deer running through the clearings, and played with the ladybirds in the grass.

As she landed on a buttercup to rest, she saw a fat, hairy caterpillar crawling towards her. "Hello!" she said. "You look all cuddly and squishy!" The caterpillar said nothing. It just wiggled its head at her.

Princess Fayette was so enchanted with the caterpillar that she picked up the leaf it was on, and carried it home with her.

"Mummy!" she sang out in front of the doorway. "Can I keep this as a pet?"

Her mother appeared at the door. "Well, of course you can," she agreed. "But you must be gentle and kind to it, and make sure it has food and drink and seems happy to live here."

Fayette clapped her hands in excitement. She made a home for her new friend, and watched it wiggle up and down the plants she gave to it, munching holes in the leaves. Every day she checked that it seemed happy, and that it had fresh plants to eat.

One morning, Fayette flew downstairs and straight outside to see the caterpillar. She looked under all the leaves, but it had gone. She sat on a toadstool and cried. Why had the caterpillar run away?

For many days, Fayette looked in the caterpillar's home to see if it had come back. Every day, she was disappointed. Still, she kept the home just as it was, and hoped her caterpillar friend would appear again.

One bright, sunny Tuesday, Princess Fayette lifted the leaves to see if her caterpillar had returned. She felt a tiny breeze on her cheek, and looked up to see what was there. A movement caught her eye, and she saw the most beautiful butterfly fluttering around her face.

Of course!

Her caterpillar hadn't run away – it had changed into a wonderful, colourful butterfly!

Rapunzel

A very poor couple had no food to feed themselves and their baby girl. They lived next to a witch, who grew wonderful food in her garden. The father decided he would try to pick something for them to eat.

The witch caught the man as he stood in her vegetable patch. "Enough!" she cried. "Give me your daughter or I will kill you all!"

The witch was not cruel to the girl, but she did keep her locked in a tall tower with no door so the girl could never escape. Every day, the witch would call from the bottom of the tower: "Rapunzel, Rapunzel, let down your hair!"

The girl had such long hair that she could unpin it and let it fall down to the ground. Then the witch would climb it like a ladder, and deliver food and drink to Rapunzel.

When the witch was away, Rapunzel filled her days by singing. A passing prince heard her marvellous voice and stopped to listen. He was amazed to see the witch calling to the girl and climbing up her long hair.

That night, the prince crept to the bottom of the tower. "Rapunzel, Rapunzel, let down your hair!" he whispered. Rapunzel was shocked to see him appear in her room, but was happy to have someone to talk to.

Every night, the prince visited Rapunzel, and soon they were in love. But the witch found out, and waited in the tower for the prince to visit.

As he climbed Rapunzel's hair, the witch took out her scissors and – snip! – cut off her long locks. The Prince tumbled into a poisoned bush and ran away, blinded.

The witch was so angry with Rapunzel that she took her to the forest and left her there.

"Rapunzel, is that you?" cried a voice. The prince staggered towards her and she kissed his poor eyes. Instantly, they were healed and he could see again. They were able to find their way back to his father's kingdom and lived happily ever after.

The Princess and the Pea

Prince Chosef was unhappy. He wanted to marry a princess, but he couldn't find one. He had travelled the whole world looking, but nobody seemed quite right. Every time he was introduced to someone new, something felt slightly wrong. He simply wasn't convinced they were true princesses.

He returned to the palace and told his parents about his problem. "Don't worry, my darling son," said his mother. "Leave it in the hands of fate."

That night, a dreadful storm blew up. The winds howled and the rain lashed down. A young girl knocked on the palace door to seek shelter for the night.

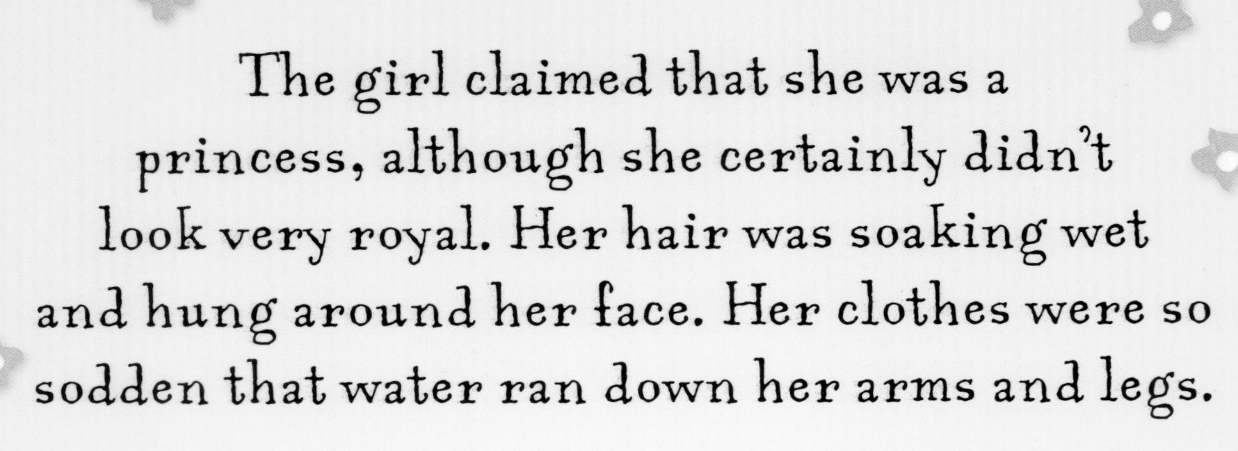

The girl claimed that she was a princess, although she certainly didn't look very royal. Her hair was soaking wet and hung around her face. Her clothes were so sodden that water ran down her arms and legs.

The queen gave the girl dry clothes, and then prepared a bed for her. She placed ten mattresses on top of each other, and hid a tiny pea at the very bottom.

The next morning at breakfast, the girl looked exhausted. "I don't know what is wrong," she sighed. "I had the biggest, squishiest bed ever, but I couldn't sleep. It felt like something was digging into me all night."

The queen took Prince Chosef by the hand and led him to the guest room. She showed him the pea. "Only a true princess would be so sensitive that this would keep her awake all night," she explained.

Prince Chosef looked at the bed and his face lit up with an enormous smile. He ran downstairs to find the princess, and asked her to become his wife.

The princess was delighted and they were soon married. They lived happily together and the princess slept soundly in their royal bed. As for the pea, it is on display in their royal museum, where all who visit can look at it and marvel at how sensitive a real princess must be.

First published 2012 by Brown Watson
The Old Mill, 76 Fleckney Road
Kibworth Beauchamp
Leicestershire LE8 0HG

ISBN: 978-0-7097-1982-3

Reprinted 2014, 2015
Printed in Malaysia
Illustrated by Gill Guile